Beauty and the Beast

Retold by Jan Carr
Illustrated by Katy Bratun

SCHOLASTIC INC.
New York Toronto London Auckland Sydney

For Steve with love
— K.B.

ISBN 0-590-46451-5

12 11 10 9 8 7 6 5 4 3 2 3 4 5 6 7 8/9

Printed in the U.S.A. 24

First Scholastic printing, October 1993

Once upon a time there lived a wealthy merchant who had three daughters. All of the daughters were pretty, but the youngest was the fairest by far. Everyone called her Beauty.

Beauty was as sweet-natured as she was sweet-faced. Not so her sisters. They spent their days shopping and their evenings at gossip. "We are the *real* beauties," they said, fluffing their gowns. The sisters were very jealous of Beauty.

One day, the father's ships were lost in a storm at sea. The family was forced to move to a small cottage deep within the forest. Now Beauty had to work hard. Still she sang as she moved about her chores. Her sisters watched her through angry eyes.

"What is there to sing about?" complained one.

"I'll sing the day we're rich again," grumbled the other.

Seasons passed. One day Beauty's father received a letter saying that one of his ships had come safely back to harbor. As he set off to the city to claim it, his two older daughters begged him to bring back presents. "New gowns!" they demanded. "And jewels!"

"All I want, Father," said Beauty, "is a single rose."

When the merchant reached the city, he found his ship damaged. All of the goods on it had spoiled, and the merchant knew he would return home as poor as he'd left.

That night, as he journeyed home, a storm swelled. Sleet and snow stung the merchant's cheeks. He heard wolves howl and feared he would die.

Then, in the distance, he noticed a warm light glimmer through the trees. It came from a great palace. Though it was winter, the gardens that surrounded the palace were in full bloom.

When the merchant knocked at the door, no one answered. He let himself in and was surprised to find a crackling fire blazing in the hearth and dinner set at a grand table. Since the merchant was hungry and cold, he sat down to eat. Afterwards, he found a bed piled high with quilts. There he slept soundly through the night.

The next morning when the merchant awoke, he found the table set with a thick wedge of bread and a warm cup of chocolate. Still, he saw no one else in the palace. In the gardens, he passed a fragrant bower of roses.

Ah, he thought, *I can at least return with a rose for Beauty*. He plucked one.

Suddenly a great, ugly beast stood before him.

"How dare you steal my roses!" roared the Beast. "Is this the way you repay me for my kindness? You must die!"

The merchant fell to his knees. "Forgive me," he whispered, "I meant no harm. This rose was a gift for my daughter."

"You have daughters?" asked the Beast. "Then you may go. But one of your daughters must agree to come and live here forever. If no daughter comes, I will hunt you down and kill you.

"Go," said the Beast. "Take this horse. It will lead you home. When the time comes, it will bring your daughter to me."

The merchant did as the Beast instructed. In an instant he was home. The poor man handed Beauty her rose. "Enjoy this rose, Beauty," he said. "This small present has cost me dearly." Then he told his children the whole horrible story.

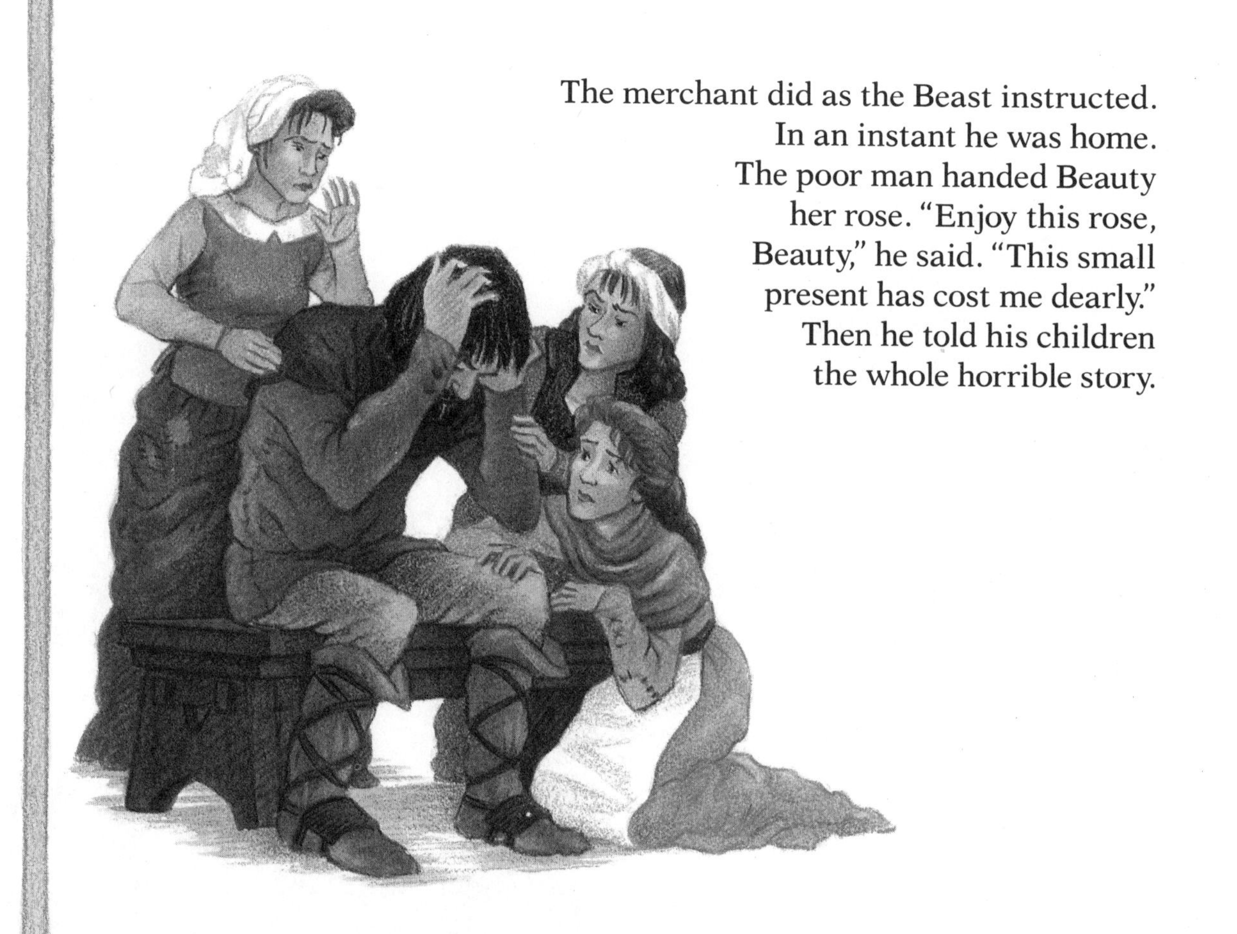

"Why did you ask for a rose?" Beauty's sisters demanded. "This is all *your* fault!"

"Then *I'll* go live with the Beast," said Beauty.

"No!" cried her father. But Beauty would not change her mind.

The next morning, she set off for the Beast's palace.

When Beauty arrived, she found a table already set for dinner. As she sat down to eat, Beauty heard the sound of footsteps on the stairs. She turned and almost cried out, for there stood the ugliest creature she had ever seen.

But he spoke to her in a gentle voice.

"Do you think that I'm ugly?" asked the Beast.

"Yes," said Beauty, who could not lie.

"Would you marry me?" asked the Beast.

"Oh no!" cried Beauty. She was surprised, though, to find that she wasn't at all afraid of the Beast.

In the days that followed, Beauty explored the palace and found it filled with everything she loved — stacks of books, music, and flowers. Anything she ever wanted appeared as if by magic.

The Beast may be ugly, but he certainly is kind to me, she thought.

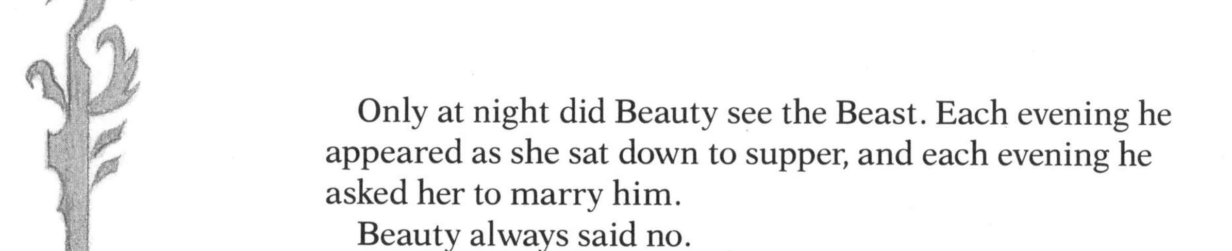

Only at night did Beauty see the Beast. Each evening he appeared as she sat down to supper, and each evening he asked her to marry him.

Beauty always said no.

Although Beauty lived happily at the palace, she began to miss her family. Finally, one night, she asked the Beast if she might return home for a visit.

The Beast looked unhappy. "You may go for a week," he said. "At the end of your visit, take off this ring and place it on the table next to your bed. If you don't come back, I will surely die."

Beauty returned to her family with a trunk of gold sent by the Beast. When her sisters saw Beauty looking more radiant than daylight and bearing such riches, they began to plot against her.

"We'll ask her to stay longer than a week," they said. "Then the Beast will be so angry that he'll *eat* her!"

A week passed. Her sisters begged her to stay, and so Beauty did.

Then one night she had a dream. She saw the Beast stretched out in the palace garden, dying. Beauty awoke frightened and crying. "How ungrateful I've been," she wept, and immediately set her ring upon the table.

When she awoke in the morning, she was back in the palace.

Beauty raced into the garden. "Beast! Beast! Where are you?" she cried. She came to a spot that looked like the one she had seen in her dream. There lay the Beast just as she had seen him. A feeling of great tenderness welled up in Beauty and she flung her arms around him. His heart was still beating!

"Oh, Beast!" cried Beauty. "I love you! You may be ugly, but you have a beautiful heart." She buried her face in his fur. "I *will* marry you," she said. "I want to be your bride."

When Beauty looked up, the Beast had disappeared, and in his place stood a handsome prince. "Long ago," he explained, "a wicked fairy put me under a spell. The spell could only be broken by someone who wanted to marry me in spite of my ugliness. You, Beauty, have freed me."

With great joy, Beauty sent for her family to celebrate her wedding. Beauty and the prince were married. Together, they lived happily ever after.